You will like this book,

... if you enjoy reading:

The writing style of *Indian Mystery* by Raleigh Minard aligns with certain hallmarks of adventure and historical fiction, particularly narratives that blend cultural elements, individual heroics, and historical backdrops. Here are a few authors and types of literature that this work could be compared to:

Zane Grey and Louis L'Amour: The depiction of Native American history, the Western frontier, and the adventurous, sometimes harsh, survival-oriented storyline has some similarities to the works of classic Western authors like Zane Grey and Louis L'Amour. Both authors wrote extensively about life in the American frontier, including encounters between Native Americans and settlers, as well as survival and personal growth amidst a rugged landscape.

James Fenimore Cooper: The storyline, which includes exploration, cultural artifacts, and themes of Native American history, is reminiscent of James Fenimore Cooper's "Leatherstocking Tales," particularly The Last of the Mohicans. Cooper's novels are characterized by similar interactions between European settlers and Native Americans, with emphasis on adventure and an understanding of cultural dynamics.

Tony Hillerman: Though Hillerman wrote more in the detective genre, his novels often feature Navajo tribal police and delve deeply into the cultural history and spiritual life of Native American communities. The inclusion of artifacts and a treasure hunt-like plot bears some resemblance to Hillerman's method of tying mystery with Native American cultural elements.

Jules Verne: The sense of adventure, hidden caves, mysterious artifacts, and suspense in "Indian Mystery" recalls elements of the adventure style made popular by Jules Verne. Although Verne's works are more in the realm of science fiction, the adventurous spirit and discovery-oriented narrative in both have notable similarities.

Mark Twain: The character of Dennis Brittan and his exploration through the wilderness, his youth, resourcefulness, and innocence, all evoke some of the tone of Mark Twain's "Tom Sawyer" or "The Adventures of Huckleberry Finn." Particularly, Dennis' adventures and narrow escapes remind one of Huck Finn's exploits along the Mississippi.

H. Rider Haggard: The emphasis on hidden treasure and long-forgotten artifacts, paired with adventurous undertones, is similar to Haggard's King Solomon's Mines. Haggard's writing style often includes lost civilizations, treasure hunts, and themes of discovery, which align well with the adventure elements in Minard's story.

Will Hobbs and Gary Paulsen: The young protagonist in "Indian Mystery" surviving in the wilderness and relying on survival skills also brings to mind more modern writers like Will Hobbs and Gary Paulsen. Works like Hatchet by Gary Paulsen deal with themes of survival, isolation, and resourcefulness, similar to Dennis' experience in the wilderness with Little Bird.

Writing Style

The narrative style also seems influenced by classic Western tropes, mixing themes of frontier life, self-reliance, and cultural conflict. The straightforward, descriptive language and emphasis on moral lessons remind me of literature designed to evoke an adventure for younger readers, often with an undertone of coming-of-age and self-discovery.

This combination of Western adventure, historical fiction, cultural conflict, and survival themes places "Indian Mystery" among works that strive to evoke the spirit of an earlier America and the complex interactions between people navigating the frontiers of their world.

Indian
Mystery

Raleigh Minard

Indian Mystery
First edition, published 2024

By Raleigh Minard

Cover design by Reprospace, LLC

Paperback ISBN-13: 978-1-952685-75-0

Published by Kitsap Publishing
Poulsbo, WA 98370
www.KitsapPublishing.com

To the storytellers of the past, who preserved the
spirit of adventure, and to the dreamers of today,
who keep those stories alive.

To the people who have shared their culture,
history, and wisdom, and to those who listen with
an open heart.

To my family, whose unwavering support turned
an idea into reality.

Thank You!

Chapter One

In the mid-eighteen hundred, Chief Joseph surrendered to the Calvary. And all the Indians of the Nez Pearce were moved to the reservation. The Shaman of that time; managed to locate and store all artifacts that have collected from over the years. There was even some gold and silver placed in the cave. Over time the new Shaman managed to devise defenses for the cave to protect the artifacts from the white man. The last Shaman hid the cave, and everyone forgot about it. The Shaman was old and needed to pass on the secrets of the talking stick and the location of the cave. But everyone in the tribe shunned the Shaman. They didn't want to hear the old stories and secrets. Most of all, no one wanted to become the next Shaman. One day the Shaman just up and left the reservation and went off into the wilderness to die. His family became disgraced before the tribe. They were forced to find the Shaman and bring back the talking stick and the secrets of the cave.

The Shaman's family managed to track him to the mountaintop where the town of Weippe was being built. There they lost his trail; they assumed that the old Shaman died, and some carrion carried away his remains. Little did they know that Old Shaman was living in a cave just down the canyon a few miles from where they chose to settle down; they continued to search for him and the talking stick. The Old Shaman dies in the cave but before he does, he carves into the talking stick the secret of the cave, and he also leaves clues on the cave wall of his home. Over time they gave up on finding the talking stick and settled down to live their lives. Little Bird's father builds a cabin in the woods, miles away from the white man settlement hoping that the white man would leave them alone. Little Bird was born not long after the cabin was built. At the age of five, she would go with her father or mother to help work on the trap lines. She learns to hunt, fish and trap small game. Then one night, the white men came to the cabin, all liquored up. And Little Bird's mom hid her away.

What follows is not pretty. The husband tries to protect his wife when he is shot in the back, then they kill the mother after using her, and they drive away, leaving the bodies lying there. The next morning Little Bird finds her parents dead. This gives her a hatred for all white men. If necessary, she will kill them for being on her land, any white man.

My name is Dennis Brittan my parents moved us from Missoula Montana to an out of the way place in Idaho called Weippe (WE' IPPE') it was the end of the summer that we moved from Montana to Idaho. I like to explore, and if I can, I love to fish. I have a gift that I keep to myself. I have a photographic memory of sorts. I cannot look at a book and remember anything, but my mind can take a picture of the landscape, or people, animals, and years later, I can sketch them as I saw them. I'm always looking for an interesting subject as I walk.

That morning I get up, the sun is shining with not a cloud in the sky. It seems that it'll be a great day. I get an early breakfast and pack up my day pack; I include a lunch some water and a few things that I was taught to include in my backpack by the Civil Air Patrol (CAP). I add my sketch pad and fishing equipment. I include a flashlight, rope, and a space blanket. I put on my hunting knife and pocket my flint and steel kit for starting fires. While exploring the small town I run onto a few boys in town. They told me about a canyon not too far from my home where I can find an underground stream coming out of the rocks, and further downstream, I can find pools full of fish. With equipment in hand, I set out in search of the canyon and the stream.

The Town of Weippe is situated on top of a mountain, and the wilderness is just outside one's back door. The population is about four hundred people, all told. It contains one mercantile, a gas station, a post office, two schools, and a park. Not much else. I start my adventure; I cross the dirt road I live next to. Then I crawl under the Barbwire fence and head south. Before I do that, I looked for a sign saying to keep out, and there are none, so I continue my hike. On the far side of the property, I come across another dirt road. I cross the road, and onto another forested area again, I look for signs to make sure I don't cause myself some problems in trespassing on other people's property.

It takes me two hours to reach the edge of the area the guys told me about. A half-hour later, I spy the clear area that marks the beginning of the canyon that I'm looking for. I walk up to the edge and see that it is the very place the guys mentioned. They didn't tell me that this place belongs to the Indians and is off-limits to people, primarily white people. I start down the canyon following a trail of sorts until I locate the waterfall coming out of the rock. I follow it down further until I find the pools of water, and sure enough, they're full of fish, nice, good-sized trout swimming facing upstream looking for food coming their way. I get my fishing pole out to try my luck. I drop my line into the water and get a nibble; the fish don't seem to be very hungry. I leave my line in the water and take out my sketchbook, and I start making a sketch of the falls and surrounding area. I couldn't have asked for a better day. The sound of the water and the fishing was great, even if I didn't catch much. I was enjoying the quiet and the landscape. As I was drawing, I started to hum one of the popular songs of the day as I continued to work on my sketch.

"Hey, You! What are you doing here?"

I almost dropped my sketch pad and pencil.

"What?" I ask.

"You don't belong here, so why are you here?"

"I'm sorry, I came in search of a fishing hole."

"I see that you found one on my people's property. You're not allowed to be here; you're trespassing on Indian land."

"I looked for a sign (s), and I didn't see one where I crossed the dirt road."

"It doesn't matter, white man, get out of here and don't return!"

"Ok, I'm leaving."

I pack up my stuff and start to head out when I see the cougar on a rock above us. I shout.

"Look out...!"

CHAPTER TWO

The Cougar pounces on the Indian girl knocking her down, causing her to hit her head on the rocks. With the Cougar now between the girl and me is hissing at me, I can see that the girl is not moving, and the Cougar is defending it's supposed kill. I take out my fishing rod and using it like a whip I hit the Cougar across the face, then he begins stalking me forgetting the girl. I try slapping the Cougar again and somehow the Cougar grabs the rod out of my hand, I see a nearby tree limb a few feet away from me. I spring for the limb. The Cougar is jumping on me, and I use the limb like a club and manage to knock the Cougar into the fast-moving stream. I watch him as he is carried downstream. Realizing the Cougar will return as soon as he gets to shore, I go over to the girl and try to wake her when I realize she's out cold. I pick her up in a fireman's carry and start up the canyon, hoping to find a place I can defend us from the Cougar. I can hear the Cougar as he is heading in our direction, the only thing in my favor is that the Cougar is on the other side of the stream so he'll have to get to the top of the canyon then come back down.

I start looking for a place I can defend, and I see a shelf overhang surrounded by boulders. I take the girl into the rocks when I discover a hidden cave. I carefully set the girl down and quickly inspect the cave to see if it is occupied, it's not, so I drag the girl further inside and set her up against a log until I have the entrance secure. I find as much wood as I can to start a fire at the entrance. With a book of matches, I'm able to start a fire fairly quickly; it appears to be just in time. The opening of the cave gets darker as the Cougar stands in the entrance growling. The Cougar tries to get past the fire but gets burned a few times and so quits. When the Cougar leaves, I turn my attention to the girl; she hasn't stirred or awaken. I get some of my water from my canteen and wash her wounded head, then using my pack as a pillow, I try to make her comfortable. I cover her with the space blanket to help keep her warm and try to keep her from shock.

There is not much I can do for the moment, so I decide to investigate the cave. As I play my light along the floor, I almost drop my flashlight. I spot a skeleton on the floor and up against a wall. I look closer and realize it has been dead for many years; it was dry and dusty looking. It appears to be wearing Indian clothes. Leggings, leather shirt, and a headband, and they had some beadwork done on them. In his hands, I saw what looked like a walking stick ornately carved with a wolf sitting on the top of the stick with strange designs down its length. I use my flashlight. On the walls and ceiling, I find unusual pictures. I carefully get my sketch pad out, and pencils and I spent the night sketching the dead Indian, the cave walls, and the Indian girl. I remove the stick from the old Indian and make a careful sketch of the stick, then place it back where I found it.

I look at my watch and see that morning is not far off, and I wonder how I'll get the girl out of here? The fire has died out, so I take a chance and leave the cave to look around. I find another club, and I peer around the rocks, then move out into the open. The Cougar is gone, for now, I can see the Cougar's tracks where he came down the canyon and then again where he returned up toward the top of the canyon. I hope the Cougar went off looking for other prey. I return to the cave and look at the girl and try to decide what to do; then, I get an idea. I take out the rope, cut it into shorter lengths, and make a backpack harness so I can carry her out with it. I wrap it around her shoulders, waste, and between her legs. Then one around her chest so I can keep her back-to-back to me. When I'm ready and have her harnessed up, I make another trip out of the cave, and I still don't see the Cougar. I carefully carry the girl out where I can hoist her onto my back. Once I have her in place, I grab my club, start up the hill with my charge on my back, and try not to fall or jar her any more than I have to.

CHAPTER THREE

Imanaged to get from the top of the hill to where I met the Indian girl in twenty minutes, now it's taking me an hour to move uphill. I concentrate on taking one step at a time, and at each pause, I listen to see if the cougar might not be near. If I would've looked up to see my progress, I would've given up. Just one step at a time, giving no thought to the next step until I have completed the one, I'm on. Not looking back either. As I walk, the cougar is ever on my mind. I strain my ears to listen for any telltale signs I'm being stalked. So far, nothing. It seems like hours when I reach the top of the canyon. I lean against a pine tree to catch my breath; I dare not sit down or I might not be able to get back up. As I stand there, I see that the cougar has been here. I also see tracks of a horse, and they lead off in the opposite direction than the dirt road. With my club in hand, I make my way to the dirt road and decide to follow it toward town to get help from a passing car. It's a mile to the road from where we are. Once again, I watch my feet as I take one step at a time. Every so often, I stop next to a tree to catch my breath and lean against it. I take out a candy bar that I had in my pack to give me some energy. Then on to the road. The whole time my charge is unconscious and does not move any at all. I hope that she'll be ok. It's for her wellbeing that drives me on.

I reach the road and am elated; now maybe I can get some help to get the girl to a hospital. I trudge down the road toward town a lady in a car drives by and doesn't stop, even with me waving my arms, she drives on by. My spirits are sagging now, and I hear another car coming down the road in our direction. I turn and wave my arms and call out for help. The man in a small pickup pulls over.

"Here son put her in the truck's back, what happened, is she dead?"

I manage with the man's help to get the girl off my back, and gently we lay her down in the truck bed.

"No, not dead, she's still breathing. She hit her head on a rock and maybe in a coma. We need her to a doctor as soon as possible."

"All right, Son, get in back with her, and I'll get us there as soon as we possibly can."

I sit with the girl, and I hold her against me, and I cover her with the space blanket to help keep her warm, and the air stream from the truck flows around us. It takes an hour to reach Orofino's town, and just up the hill is where the hospital is. We pull up to the Emergency Room entrance, and the man driving the truck runs in to get help. Then returns with a couple of nurses and a gurney. They carefully load the girl on to it, wheel her away into a room, and start working on her.

I retreat to the waiting room, where I can call my mom to let her know I'm fine. Mr. Dallas is there, and I thank him for his help.

"Son, how are you getting home?"

"I'm called my mom; she'll be frantic that I didn't return home last night."

"I'll see you when school starts in a few weeks" said Dalles.

"Are you a teacher?" I ask.

"As a matter of fact, yes, I'm the shop teacher. You'll have to tell me your story about what happened. I want to commend you on your harness set up, where did you learn to do that?"

"I was in the CAP (Civil Air Patrol) in Montana for a year, and a survival instructor showed us how to do that."

Mr. Dallas shakes my hand and must get home himself.

Chapter Four

I dial the phone and call my mother, "Hi, Mom."

"WHERE ARE YOU!?"

"I'm at the hospital in Orofino."

"WHAT!"

"I'm fine, mom I'm not hurt, a girl I met fell and hit her head, and I had to carry her to the road to get help. A cougar had attacked her."

"Are you ok, Dennis?"

"Mom, I'm fine, just exhausted; I'll tell you all about it later. Can you come and get me?"

"I'll be there in a while after I call your stepfather to let him know where I'm going."

"Thank you, mom."

I hang up the phone; Mr. Dallas had not left yet.

"How was the phone call?"

"About what I expected, I've a feeling my explanations will not be believed, and the punishment will not be pretty."

"What is your name?"

"I'm sorry, Mr. Dallas, my name is Dennis, Dennis Brittan."

"Well, Dennis, it was a brave thing you did, and if you like, I'll talk to your parents to let them know what you did."

"I'd appreciate that."

Dallas leaves and wishes Dennis well. I sit down in the chair to wait and promptly fall asleep. In mid snore, a Doctor wakes me up.

"Hunh…wha… Yes," said, Dennis

"What is your name?"

"Dennis."

"Well, Dennis, what can you tell me about the girl you brought in?"

I stretch and yawn, then I relate the story about the cougar, and how it knocked her down, and how I managed to push the cougar into the fast-rushing stream. Then was forced into a small cave to protect the girl and myself. Then how I got us out of there in the morning.

"Did you know the girl?"

"No, I was trying to get her name and give her mine when the cougar pounced on her."

"So, you do not know her, or her parents?"

"No. Doctor, how is she?"

"She's in a coma; these things can be very tricky. She might be like this for days or years. All we can do is keep her comfortable, and it would help if someone would talk to her or even read to her."

"Could I be allowed to do that?"

"Well, right now, you're the nearest relative she has for the moment. Until we find her parents."

"Thank you, Doctor."

Mom shows up and is about to go into a tirade when Doctor Fox pulls her aside and tells her the courageous thing that Dennis did. The doctor takes her to the girl's room and shows her the person he saved. Mom has a change in heart at that point. She asks the doctor if she can take me home now, and he agrees. On the way, mom wants the whole story, so I relate the story about the hike, the stream, and the Indian girl: the cougar and a small cave. To date, I have told no one about the skeleton and the cave markings. I have decided to tell the girl only in case there may be some Indian taboo against people knowing of it. On the drive home, I try to get mom to permit me to visit the girl at the hospital. And all she would say is to ask your father. I give up and decide to sleep on the way home.

Chapter Five

Mom wakes me up after we get home, and I go to the kitchen and make a peanut butter sandwich; I realize I haven't eaten since breakfast yesterday. Fortified with a glass a milk and my sandwich, I drop off to sleep. The next thing I remember is my stepdad waking me up.

"Oh, hi, Shorty (His Nick Name)."

"I hear you had quite an adventure yesterday."

"Yes, sir, I did."

"I also heard from your mother that you want to ask me for a favor?"

"Yes, I do."

"What is it?"

By his tone of voice, I can tell it could go one way or another, either for me or against me.

"The Doctor said the girl, might recover sooner if some would visit her and talk or read to her. I feel responsible for her situation. I need to be the one to do it."

"How're you going to get there?" asks Shorty.

"I don't plan on going every day, just every couple of days. I know you go that way quite often. If it would be ok, with you. Could I hitch a ride with you down to Orofino? And hitchhike back?"

"Let me think about this, and I'll get back to you, Dennis."

I let it go at that, to badger Shorty would bring an instant No. I'll let him think it over, a lot of times he surprises me with his decisions.

The next day, I get ready to hike back to the canyon's head and follow the horse tracks. I travel back there, in hopes that I can find her parents. I locate the tree where the horse was tied up, and I see both the horse tracks and the cougar tracks, and I follow them. An hour into the hike from the canyon head, I spy an old log cabin. I walk up with caution, not knowing if I might be shot or not. I knock on the door, and no one answers. I look around and find that the horse made it home. I see that the horse still has a saddle on it, so I carefully walk up to it and start taking the saddle off, and I put the saddle on the pole fence in the barn. I see several other animals, Chickens, a few goats, and a cow. I also know that they need to feed a watered, so I roll up my sleeves and set to work. I move some hay out of the loft, then I see a hand pump for water, and I fill up the trough and a large barrel.

I enter the house when I finish the chores I had outside, and I see things that need to be cleaned up, so I do them, I run on to a picture of the Indian girl, and it says her name is Little Bird. The house doesn't have any power and no phone. I take some paper to leave a note for her parents explaining where I live and where their daughter is. I leave to return home. That's when I see the two graves with flowers on them. I figure out that these are her parents. I return home, being careful not to run into the cougar who may be lurking about. When I reach home, Shorty wants to talk to me.

"You may go see the girl, I feel if you are big enough to shoulder the responsibility of getting her to the hospital, then you are responsible enough to see this through. For now, you have to make sure to get your chores done around here before you can go, and you will have to hitchhike home. I may be able to do something about that in the not-too-distant future, we'll see."

I about bust a gut thanking him, I do my chores here at home because tomorrow I'll need to be ready to go with Shorty as he heads off to a job in the woods at St. Marie's, which means I'll have to hitchhike home.

We leave at three-O-clock in the morning, and Shorty drops me off at the hospital. It's very early, like four–O-clock in the morning. I go to the waiting room and sit down and go to sleep. I manage to get in a few hours when Doctor Fox is waking me up.

CHAPTER SIX

"Dennis, wake up."

"Sorry I was tired. Little Bird has no parents; they died a several years ago."

"How do you know this?"

"I went back to the canyon head and found she has a horse and so I followed the tracks, where I located a cabin. I knocked, and no one answered. I found some livestock in need of being feed and water. I even cleaned up around her cabin. That's when I found the graves."

"I see. Well, Dennis, go to her room and talk to her, reading helps too. Here at the hospital, we can keep her body alive, but not her mind. She'll have a better chance of recovery if someone cares."

"Thanks, Doctor Fox. I'll get right on it."

I enter Little Bird's room and start talking to her, I tell her what happened at the canyon, and I tell her about her animals, and they're being taken care of. Then I read to her from one of the books my sisters like to read. Hardy Boys, Nancy Drew, and a few of the musher love stories. *(Not that I wanted to read such nonsense)* During some of my conversations, I take out my sketch pad and draw some of the nurses, and Doctor Fox, who I found out is a Blackfoot

Indian from Flathead Lake in Montana. In my other sketchbook, on the days I cannot come to the hospital, I return to the cave and sketch the wall paintings, and the walking stick, which I will learn, is a talking stick.

On one of my trips to the cave, I bring my camera outfit to better document what I've seen. I take several pictures of each area of the cave, and when I get some time, I will process the film. The coma drags on, and I have to go to school, so I'm only allowed to visit on Saturdays.

Shorty came home one day after working in the woods, Shorty called me out to his truck to help him unload a motorcycle; I help get it down and wheel it over to the side of the house. Then he hands me a helmet. Now you don't have to hitchhike back home.

"Really! I can use a motorcycle?"

"I bought it from someone who wants a bigger sized motorcycle, and I thought you can now get there and back on your own. I think you are man enough."

I surprise myself as I pick up Shorty and dance around with him in my arms.

"Hey, let me down. I guess this meets you approve?"

"Yes, Oh, Yes. Thank You!"

"There are some ground rules, no taking it to school if your grades drop, no motorcycle. As to the gas, I have an account set up for you. I believe in what you are doing. This is my way of helping. Don't forget your chores."

"Thank you, Shorty; I'll follow the rules I really will."

Summer has ended, and fall starts. I'm in school, and when winter gets here, I'll not be using the motorcycle. It has been two months, and Little Bird still shows no signs of recovery. It's Saturday morning, and I spend a cold ride down the mountain to Orofino. I park my motorcycle and go into the hospital, and I'm directed down the hall to Little Bird's room. I tell Little Bird about my days in class and homework, how her animals are doing. Then I break out the latest mystery novel and start reading it.

CHAPTER SEVEN

s I'm reading, Little Birds wakes up and then sits up.

"Who… You are that Boy! Who was trespassing on my property! What are you doing here! How did I get here? What have you done to me? Get out of here!"

I grab my stuff in the tirade's face and beat a hasty retreat from her room, and I sit in the waiting room; in passing, I tell the nurse the Little Bird is awake. The nurse calls the doctor and has an intern see too Little Bird and keep her in bed. Doctor Fox walks into Little Bird's room.

"Now, young lady, let's check you over."

"How'd I get here? What's wrong with me, and who let that teenage boy in my room. I hate him!"

"I think you should reconsider that. Dennis is the reason you're alive at this moment. If you want the story of what happened, you're going to have to ask him yourself. I can tell you some things about Dennis; he is very talented and brave."

"Doctor, how brave is it to attack a girl by herself in nowhere?"

"What makes you think he attacked you, and for what reason?"

"He was on my property, and I caught him there."

"Then, why save you? He could have left you there and gone home. Then you would've died, and no one would've known or cared."

Little Bird considers what the doctor says.

"Ok, send Dennis in, I'll let him tell me what happened at the canyon."

Doctor Fox tells Dennis to return to Little Bird's room, but before the doctor leaves, he shakes my hand and tells me.

"Dennis, this was a good thing you did, and because of you, Little Bird has recovered; I want to thank you. And thank you for the pictures, the nurses, and I approve of them. Anytime you want to come back and visit us, please do. I just wanted to let you know we consider you part of our staff."

"Thank you, Doctor Fox."

I gather up my stuff and decide to face the lion in her den. I knock on her door, and she said to enter. I walk into the room and put my stuff down and take a chair.

"I hear you saved my life, is that true."

"I suppose so."

"Well…"

"Well, what Little Bird?"

"Are you going to tell me what happened?"

"Yes, now where to start."

CHAPTER EIGHT

I tell Little Bird of all that happened and about the cave and how I got her out there. She didn't believe me until I told her about what I had found in the cave, and I brought out my sketchbook and showered her the drawings of the cave and the skeleton. What got her the most excited was the walking stick. Little Bird corrected me and said, "Talking Stick."

"Did you leave all that you found in the cave?" Asked Little Bird.

"Yes, everything is still there, and I haven't told anyone but you about this find. I wasn't sure if some taboo which might not be in force here."

"Yes, and no. It's a cave my family has been looking for; for some time. How did you find it?"

"When I was carrying you up the canyon, I knew the cougar would be on us at any time, so I looked for a place I could defend when I saw an overhang with rocks surrounding it. So, I entered it with you and found a cave. The rest you now know."

"When I get out of here, you'll need to show me where it is."

"I would be glad to, what is important about this discovery?"

Little Bird relates the story about her great grandfather, who was a shaman for their tribe. When he tried to get someone to replace him, no one wanted to listen; everyone was too busy trying to be like the white man. So, he disappeared into the wilderness taking the talking stick with him and the treasure cave's secret.

"You see, Dennis; the talking stick leads us to where my ancestors put a lot of our artifacts for the future. When he up and left, this disgraced his family, so we followed Grandfather here and lost his trail."

"Little Bird, let me go talk to Doctor Fox, and I'll see when you'll be leaving, now that you're awake."

I leave Little Bird in her room with my sketchbook, so she can look over the pictures I did of the cave. I locate Doctor Fox (he is a Black foot Indian from Montana) and ask when Little Bird will be ready to leave?

"Dennis, she is pretty week and will need a couple of days here so we can assess her physically and mentally. I could arrange for her to be discharged on Friday. Do you know anyone who can get her home safely?"

"Yes, Sir Doctor Fox, I'll talk my mom into it."

"Good, then I'll see you on Friday at Three-O-clock to pick her up. And I may have a surprise for you as well."

Dennis runs off to tell Little Bird what Doctor Fox told him. Several miles to the north, a robbery is taking place at an Indian museum, and most of the artifacts are stolen. No one knows who did it, and it appears to be an inside job; the building wasn't broken into. The items were taken in the very early hours of the night; no one was seen. All they found were some tire tracks leading away from a side door of the Museum. A person of interest is a man called Running Water; he was in charge of the Museum and was recently discharged when he was caught stealing artifacts.

Dennis had to leave Little Bird; he had to get home to do his promised chores and get his homework done. Little Bird asks Dennis if he would leave his sketches with her so she can study them. That night while Little Bird slept, Doctor Fox barrows Dennis's sketchbook and takes them to the copier in the back room and copies the sketches. Dr. Fox will show them to a friend of his in hopes he can get Dennis a scholarship to an art college.

Dennis is incredible at his drawing. Doctor Fox was having dinner with a friend of his, and a gourmet one at James Johnson mansion (A lawyer). Doctor Fox takes Dennis's sketches to his friend's house to show him how talented Dennis is, and see if the Lawyer would like to sponsor Dennis at an art school. Doctor Fox knocks at the door of his friend's house, and instead of the butler opening the door, James opens the door to welcome his friend.

"Good to see you, old friend, please come into my humble abode, dinner is nearly ready."

"It's so kind of you James, to have me over. I like your house, and not to mention the repast you provide me each time I come. I look forward to your invitations to come and dine with you."

"Your kind to say so, Dr. Fox, I look forward to our evening conversations. I hear that you had a small medical wonder at the hospital today."

"How did you find that out, James?"

"Let's just say I have my resources, and good news travels fast."

"It is good news, and I'd like to discuss it with you after dinner."

"Well, good doctor, I look forward to our conversation then."

Doctor Fox looks around the dining area.

"James, I see you have gotten some more artifacts; how do you go about getting them?"

"I have a few friends who let me in on a few good buys from time to time. But I have to be careful I have been sold the occasional fake. James laughs. One of them even had been made in China written on the bottom. So, you can see I'm an easy mark sometimes at collecting things."

A small bell rings.

"Doctor, our meal is about to be served, please sit down."

The meal is served, and some conversation is bandy about the usual weather, news, and the like. At the end of the meal, the Lawyer leads Doctor Fox to the library for brandy, and they sit in big comfortable chairs, enjoying the time together.

"Now, Doctor, what did you want to discuss with me?"

Doctor Fox takes a couple of sketches out of his bag, one of himself and one of the cave drawings.

Chapter Nine

"James, I have run onto a very talented young man who made these sketches."

Dr. Fox hands over the sketches to James. James takes out a magnifying glass to look at them.

"These are quite good, especially the picture of you, my good doctor."

"His name is Dennis Brittan, and he lives in Weippe, and the girl, Little Bird's recovery, is primarily because of him. Dr. Fox relates how Dennis saved the girl from a cougar attack and then managed to get them to the hospital, saving the girl's life. I know you sponsor talented people from time to time. I'm asking you if you'd do the same for Dennis."

"I might be willing to do that. I want to meet this young man, is that possible?"

"For sure, he'll be at the hospital this Friday to pick up Little Bird and return her home at three-O-clock in the afternoon."

James holds up both pictures and asks, "May I keep these?"

"I don't see why not. They're just copies."

"Very Good Doctor, I'll be there to meet the boy."

"Well, James, I must be going. I have an early call tomorrow at the hospital. Thank you for the diner, and for considering the sponsorship."

Dr. Fox shakes James Hand and leaves.

James walks over to the window and watches Dr. Fox drive off.

From a side door in steps, an Indian named; Running Waters.

"Waters, look at this sketch, is this real?"

Running Waters studies the picture very closely.

"James, this looks authentic; I'm not a master of the Nez Pierce tribe per se, but looking at this cave drawing. I'd be inclined to say it's real. It calls to mind a story I heard a few years back about an old shaman who disappeared into the wilderness with a talking stick which led the way to a treasure trove of the tribe's artifacts and possibly some gold and silver."

"Friday, I'll be meeting with the young man who drew this, and I may get some answers out of him. I'll have to be careful how I ask him I don't want to raise suspicion."

"Jim, I have the stuff in your back room that we took from the Museum; when are you shipping it out?"

"The buyer will be here in the morning to pick up the stuff and will pay me then. I'll split the money with you and the Sheriff tomorrow evening at this time."

"We'll be here, Jim."

Running Water left out the back door and drove away. Friday morning rolls around, and Dennis is on pins and needles the whole day; I'm not sure what bothers me more. Picking up Little Bird or my mother meeting Little Bird for the first time. Mom pulls into the parking lot, and we enter the hospital to pick up Little Bird. She's dressed and ready to go when we get there, but the nurse holds us up until Doctor Fox appears. Doctor Fox has a distinguished gentleman with him.

"Dennis, I'd like to introduce to you James Johnson, he's a lawyer, and when he runs across talented people, he likes to help them. I've asked him here to see you about a scholarship for your sketches."

James holds up a copy of the sketch of the cave I made and asks, if I have more drawings, I can show him. I pull out my sketchbook with the staff's pictures that I drew, and Jim asks if I have any more pictures of the cave. I lie and tell him that that is the only drawing I made. Then he asks about if I found anything else in the cave. Again, I lie and tell him no, just the painting.

"Well, Son, I may have a place for you and your skills. Then James turns to Little Bird; you must be the damsel that was in distress. How pretty you are. Well, Dr. Fox, I have a court case to get to. Dennis, it was very nice to meet you. I will get back to you."

Chapter Ten

James departs and heads to the parking lot and gets into his car, and drives off.

Mom was frowning at me, but said nothing until we get to our car.

I put Little Bird's stuff into the trunk along with my backpack, and I get into the back seat, and Little Bird gets into the back with me.

Mom asks the question. "Dennis, why did you lie to James?"

"How did you know I was lying? Mom."

She gives me her look that says I know when you are telling a lie.

"I'm not sure, but something about him, I felt like I was shaking hands with a used car salesman. I get a bad feeling about him."

"What do you mean, Dennis?" asks Little Bird.

"If he were interested in my sketches, then the ones I gave him would have satisfied him, but he keeps at me for more drawings of the cave and anything else in the cave, that's when I got suspicious."

"Now that you mention it, you may be right." Said Mom, and Little Bird agreed.

Mom drives us to our house, and I take our stuff out of the trunk and put it into the house. Of course, Little Bird gets mobbed by my sisters; they are curious about this mysterious girl who has captured their older brother's attention. Fortunately, Mom intervenes.

"Girls leave her alone. She just got out of the hospital. Let the poor girl have a little peace. Maybe later, she can chat with you when she is more comfortable."

"Thank you, uh, Mrs. Brittan."

"No, Dear. I'm Mrs. Byers, but if you like, you may call me mom, as long as my son has been going to see you. In my mind, you have become part of the family."

"Thank you." Stammers Little Bird.

"I hope you don't mind staying here tonight; it's too late to take you home, especially with the cougar between here and your home." said, Dennis.

"I understand."

"So how about we go for a walk, and I can show you around our house?"

"Ok."

I could tell Little Bird was uncomfortable with all of my family; to her, they were nice enough, but she's not used to having anyone around. For the most part, I had a shadow for the rest of the day. Little Bird wouldn't let me get more than a dozen steps from her. It was not long, and Little Bird asked if we could sit; this was more exercise than she has had in a few months. So, we sat out in the back-area side by side.

"You're going to take me home tomorrow, aren't you?"

"I sure will, and after a couple of days, when you are stronger, I'll take you to the cave."

"Sure, it has been there this long, I guess it can wait a little longer. Dennis, you're not like other white people I've known. I always hated white men! They killed my family and would've killed me, too, if I hadn't been hidden. Why did you save me?"

"You were a responsibility."

'Is that how you see me as a responsibility?"

"I did at first; now I want to be responsible for you always. I fell in love with you along the way."

"Love me? An Indian girl!"

"That's funny; you say that. I got the same reaction from my peers at school."

I look Little Bird in the eyes, and I take her hand. "Yes, it's true. I love you."

Little Bird pulls back her hand and blushes a bright red.

"I think we should go back to your house now. Won't your mother have dinner ready?"

I lead us back to the house, where mom is just about to call us for dinner.

Dinner is a simple fare stew and biscuits, and it's good. Little Bird even went back for seconds.

After dinner, I get to wash the dishes; after all, it's my turn to do them this week. Little Bird offers to help me. And it doesn't take long to get them cleaned up and put away. Little Bird lets my sisters carry her away into their bedroom. And I don't see her for the rest of the night. I get up early the next morning and pack up a lunch for both Little Bird and myself so that I can take her home. As I finish packing the backpack Little Bird finds me in the kitchen.

Chapter Eleven

"Are your sisters always so chatty?"

"More than you know, at the moment, they're cooking up a scheme to get us married."

"WHAT!"

"Don't worry about it; it's just the way they are, and no one pays them any mind."

"Good, let's get out of here."

I laugh, and Little Bird blushes again.

"Do you know you look rather cute when you blush like that?"

She slugs me in the shoulder and says, "Stop it."

I take up the pack and the canteen of Water, and we set out for her home. I take it in easy stages so that she won't tire out so quickly. In two hours, we reach the road. What either of us failed to notice is that we picked up a tail that is following us. Whoever he is, he's very quiet and stays out of sight. We cross the road, and I lead us to a stump that has been there for many years. It's large enough for us to sit on and have our lunch, which allows Little Bird to rest from the walking.

"Dennis, where's the cave?"

"It's a way down the canyon not far from where you found me. It would be too hard to tell you how to find it, so I'll show you instead."

"When?"

"How about a week? It'll give you time to recover and build up your strength; it's quite a climb down and then back up."

"I'm anxious to see the cave where my grandfather died and collect the talking stick."

"If you like, I can get the stick for you tomorrow and bring it to your home."

"No, Dennis, I want to go with you."

"It's Saturday today, so next Saturday, how about I come by and pick you up and take you there."

"OK, it's a date." She takes my hand. And now I'm the one to blush.

In another hour, we make it to her house, and she goes to check on the animals, and they're glad to see us both. This surprises Little Bird, as she watches the Horse and goat come up to me and butt me with their head. She sees that I've taken care of them as good or better than she could've and is a little jealous of the attention they are giving me.

"Please come inside my cabin and sit with me before you go."

"I'd love to."

They enter her cabin, and I sit at the table on one side and Little Bird on the other.

"You were right, Dennis; I couldn't make the trip today. Next Saturday would be best. I'm tired from our walk here."

"I can see that. Are you going to be able to feed your animals? If not, I can do it for you."

"Thanks, Dennis; after a short rest, I'll be able to do it myself."

I look at my watch and see that it is getting on, so I take my leave of Little Bird and offer to come back tomorrow.

"No, Dennis, I need to take care of myself."

"OK, but I wasn't thinking of my need to help you; I just wanted to be with you."

Little Bird blushes. "If you want to come to see me in a few days, that would be nice."

I shake her hand and leave; before I go, I leave my sketchbook of the cave for Little Bird to look at some more. I head for home. On the way, I feel as if I'm being watched and followed. The Cougar comes to mind, and I quicken my pace to be out in the open, and I take out my twenty-two pistol and check to see that it's loaded. I press on toward home. What I didn't know is that Running Water followed Little Bird and myself to her cabin, and he listened in on the conversation. And he knows that Dennis is the only one who knows where the cave is. Running Water follows Dennis to see where he goes.

Dennis gets to the road and sees a big dark blue car parked down from where he and Little Bird crossed the road. I walk to the car and look inside and see nothing. At first, I assume it's broken down, and I continue toward home. Running Water follows me all the way to my home. Something is not right, so I get on my motorcycle and head into town. Then I take the road that borders on Little Bird's property. The car is gone. I didn't see it on the way there, Running Water had just driven down the road when he saw me coming on my motorcycle, and he was just over the hill and out of sight. I pull off the road onto Little Bird's property and drive to her cabin. She comes out with a shotgun; she wasn't expecting anyone. I pull up and take off my helmet, and she lowers her gun.

"What's wrong, Dennis?"

"I saw a Blue Car on the road; it looks like one I have seen recently. I had a bad feeling. I wanted to make sure you're OK."

"I'm fine; no one has been here since you left."

"I'd feel better if you were to come home with me and stay the night again."

"No, Dennis, I couldn't handle your sisters badgering me about you again."

"I understand, and I'll wage my mother is a hand full as well."

"I didn't want to say it, but yes."

"I understand, my mom wants me to find a steady girlfriend, and I think she believes you're it."

"Even if I'm an Indian?"

"That wouldn't bother her, she wants grandchildren, and I'm the oldest."

Little Bird is speechless and blushing.

"You do know you're cute when you do that?"

"Do what?"

"Blush, like that."

"I never…"

Chapter Twelve

"You know, I may have to give that some serious consideration about asking you to be my steady girlfriend."

"I think you better go Dennis."

"I'll see you in two days, Little Bird."

While I was talking to Little Bird; Running Water drove away to Orofino to see Jim Johnson and report on what he's found out about the cave and the talking stick.

I start up the motorcycle and drive home, and I've a lot on my mind. Not so much on Little Bird, but the blue car. Something about it, in the back of my mind I saw that car before. Two days later, Little Bird meets me at the edge of her property, and I'm walking in instead of using my motorcycle.

"Hi, Little Bird, are you ready to go to the cave?"

"That's all I've been able to think about Dennis, let's go."

I take the lead, and we start down the trail toward the canyon. I take out my gun and make sure it's loaded.

"You're not going to shoot the cougar with that little gun, are you?"

"No, but he's afraid of the noise. While I was taking care of your animals, the cougar snatched a chicken, and I saw the remains. The next day the cougar appeared and was about to take another one; when I grabbed your shotgun and shot him in the face. The sting of the birdshot and the noise keeps him away from your home now. If we run on to him, my gun may frighten him away."

"If you say so, Dennis."

We get to the head of the canyon and start down into it. Forty minutes later, we reach the cave.

"Little Bird, we're here. Do you see the cave?"

"No, where is it?"

"It's right there." Dennis points to the rock overhang.

"I don't see it, Dennis."

"Follow me." Dennis leads the way to the overhang then into the cave.

As I lead the way, it appears I'm walking into a wall of rock, and I disappear; I turn around and stick my head out.

"Are you going to follow?"

Little Bird follows me into the cave; I take out my flashlight and shine it around the cave.

"This is where I laid you when I brought you in here. The skeleton is over there, and the wall painting is up there."

Little Bird has me shine it on the skeleton so she can see the talking stick, and under her breath, I hear her sing a little song; it is too low for me to make out. Then she takes up the talking stick.

"I need to get this back to my house and then to the Nez Pearce Indian Reservation," says Little Bird.

"Do you mind if I walk you home?"

"You don't need to, Dennis."

"I know, but I want to."

"Why?"

"Because I care about you, and I have a bad feeling about this. I want to know that you're safe."

"Ok, you've taken care of me this far, and I don't mind your company."

They both climb up out of the canyon, then we hear.

"Stop right there, both of you, or we'll shoot. Now put up your hands."

We put up our hands, and a man I saw in Orofino as the Sheriff walks over and takes my gun and the talking stick; he also takes my backpack with some of the sketches. He backs away, and at the edge of the bushes, another man steps out with a rifle, and they turn to walk away towards the road. At the highway, Jim meets the Sheriff and Running Water.

"I see you got the talking stick. Did you also get the sketchbook? We may need the information it holds."

"It's all right here," says the Sheriff.

"Before we go, let's take a look at the cave." Says Jim

"Why, we have the sketches," says Running Water.

"True, but you never know if you have all the data you may need until it is too late. Besides, we have both kids they're right here, and they can show us the way?" said Jim.

They make Little Bird, and Dennis gets up.

"Now, boy, show us the cave."

"No!"

Running Water grabs Little Bird and holds a gun to her head.

Jim tells Dennis, "Boy, he will kill her if you don't show us; Running Water shoot her in the leg."

Running Water cocks the pistol and starts to squeeze the trigger.

"Ok, I'll take you."

"I knew I could count on you to be sensible, Dennis. Now let's show Uncle Jim the cave."

"No, don't do it, Dennis; they'll kill us anyway." Little Bird struggles with her captor.

That was running in my mind as well, and the cave would be where we would be left for dead, and no one would be able to find us. But for now, we're alive; maybe we'll get lucky.

"Little Bird, it'll be ok; you need to trust me."

The Sheriff is right behind me, with a gun to my back, pushing me on. Luck, good or bad, was with us; up above us, I saw the cougar trailing us. I lead everyone past the cave to the same point where the cougar jumped Little

Bird and me months ago. The cougar was on cue. He let out a scream and pounces on the Sheriff, scaring Jim into dropping to the ground. Knocking Running Water off-balance, and Little Bird pushes Running Water into the fast-moving stream; I dance around the Sheriff and the cougar and grab Little Bird's hand and pull her along back up the canyon toward the cave. Before we can get there, I hear a gun go off, and the cougar runs away, but not before the Sheriff is badly injured. I pull Little Bird into the cave, and we sit to wait out the bad guys.

Chapter Thirteen

Unless you know what to look for, you can never find the cave, and with all the rocks around, there are no tracks to follow either. Soon we hear the men passing by us.

"Jim, we need to get me to a doctor; I'm bleeding pretty bad here."

The men climb back up out to the canyon to head for the car. Little Bird and I wait several minutes, and we follow them. Back at the top of the canyon, we see the men struggle along toward the road, and we keep to the trees.

The Cougar that was following little Bird, and I was not far off. We trailed the bad guy back to the road.

I call out, "Jim, we will tell the authorities about this."

Jim takes the rifle from Running Water and shoots at me, and manages to hit me in the leg, making me fall to the ground. The noise scares the Cougar away before we even knew it was there. The men get into the car and turn around on the road and drive off to Orofino, leaving us behind.

Little Bird takes off my shirt and makes a bandage for me to stop the bleeding. Then she helps me over to the edge of the road.

"You foolish boy, why did you have to say anything they would've left without shooting at us?"

"I wanted them to know I'm going to stop them."

"I'm going to have to leave you here to go get help. Will you be Ok?"

"Give me that stick so that I can protect myself. Then go get help."

Little Bird gets Dennis the stick and then sets off at a run towards Dennis's house. Forty minutes later, Little Bird is banging on the door to my house and shouting she needed help. Mom opens the door and asks.

"What do you need, Little Bird?"

"Dennis was shot, and I had to leave him next to the road; we have to hurry. The Cougar may still be around."

Mom grabs her keys and purse and leads the way to the car. Once seated, mom asks,

"Which way do we go?"

Little Bird tells her to go to the gas station on the edge of town; mom guns the car, and they're there in just minutes, then she guides her down the dirt road towards her property. They soon find Dennis sitting there, and not far away, a wary cougar crouched ready to spring. Mom pulls her twenty-two pistol out of her purse and fires a couple of shots into the air causing the Cougar to run off.

Both Little Bird and mom help me to the car and get me seated in the back seat. Seeing how pale I look, mom guns it to Orofino to the hospital, and we make it in record time. When we get there, Doctor Fox is summoned to the ER to look at me, and soon they remove the bullet and bandage me up. And put me in a room to wait; I found out later that they call the Sheriff's office to report a shooting. Dr. Fox comes into my room to talk to me.

"Who shot you?"

"James Johnson, Running Water, and the Sheriff here in town."

"What?"

"Yes, they tried to get me to show them the cave, and they took the talking stick from Little Bird. I need to get out of here before they show up."

"Doctor Fox, what Dennis said is true," said Little Bird.

"Where is your mother, Dennis?"

"She is in the waiting room."

"I'll get her and be back."

Fox goes to the nurse and tells her, "when the Sheriff or the deputy gets here, send him to room ten."

"But doctor, there is no one in that room."

"Nurse does as I ask; I'll explain later."

"Ok, doctor."

Doctor Fox gets my mom, rushes her to my room, and then gets me into a wheelchair.

"Mrs. Byers, go get your car and come to this back door; we need to get you all out of here now."

Mom senses the urgency in his voice and does what he says. Dr. Fox helps to load me into the car, and the women get in with me.

"You must get out of here. Your lives are in danger if you stay here; I will come to your house tomorrow to see how Dennis is doing. Here are some antibiotics and a few painkillers. I'll see you tomorrow."

Chapter Fourteen

"I'm doing fine, Dr. Fox."

"You're up and out of bed?"

"I feel fine, is there a problem?"

"Yes, you were right, Jim seems to be mixed up in several thefts centered on Indian artifacts, and I need you and Little Bird to come with me to the Indian reservation."

"Why does my son and Little Bird have to go with you?" asks mom.

Little Bird is a bit shocked; no one has ever stood up for her before except her mother.

"Look, if you want to, you can come along, but I'll need them to identify these people for the law. Dennis, do you still have your sketchbook?"

"No, they took it. How about I go one better? I took pictures of everything and had them in my notebook under my bed."

"You took pictures of the cave and the talking stick? That's great, Dennis."

"Yes, I took pictures; besides, I could re-do all my sketches in detail. I have a photographic memory."

I turn to Little Bird, "Could you please go get the notebook just under my bed."

Little Bird looks at me, then runs to the bedroom and brings back the wrong notebook.

"No, this is not the right one; it says Indian mystery on it."

Fox puts a hand on my shoulder and shakes his head; then I get it.

"Scott, please get the notebook. Thanks!"

Scott returns with the book, and I open it up to show Dr. Fox and Little Bird the pictures I took, especially the talking stick.

"Jim and his group have returned to Orofino. I saw them as I was coming here. That talking stick that Jim has. He was examining it when I drove by. We must get to the Nez Pearce Indian reservation before they do."

"Mom, Shorty, I'll be Ok, going with Doctor Fox; after all, he could have turned me over to the sheriff deputy, but he didn't."

"You may go," said Shorty.

Chapter Sixteen

om was about to protest, but Shorty stopped her with a look.

"Dennis, you have gotten this far on your adventure; you just as well go the rest of the way. I think you are brave enough to see this through. Now one thing for me. Don't get killed, or I will never hear the end of it."

I take Shorty's hand in a firm handshake and thank him. Then Scott and Doctor Fox help me out to Fox's car and into the back seat. Little Bird is hovering all around me, making sure I'm not being hurt, and she is holding on to the book; when I'm all in the car, mom kisses my forehead and wishes me well. To my shock, Little Bird kisses me full on the lips, and we both blushes. She gets into the front seat with Doctor Fox, and we head down the road. It takes a good four hours to get to the Nez Pearce Indian Reservation. Dr. Fox stops at the entrance and gets permission to go to the hospital where his college friend Doctor Tall Elk works.

Dr. Fox helps me out of the car, gets me a pair of crutches, and helps me into the clinic. At the nurse's station, Dr. Fox asks if Dr. Tall Elk is free to talk to him. The nurses call Dr. Tall Elk, and he comes out dressed for surgery.

"Dr. Fox, you are arriving at the most opportune time. I need you to perform this surgery; here, look at this chart."

"I see, this is very serious, I'll come with you, Dr. Tall Elk, and when this is over, I have a rather lengthy story for you to hear."

Fox turns to Little Bird and me, "you guys will have to wait here; I must do this surgery now; I will return in a few hours."

We don't see Dr. Fox for a few hours. In the meantime, we get hungry, so I ask the nurse where we might get something to eat. She looks at me then points to the vending machines down the hall. It's not what I had in mind, but Little Bird and I go there, and I buy a package of sandwiches and a couple of milk containers. I would've bought more, but I ran out of money. I shared my meal with Little Bird, and she smiles at me for it. When we were eating Jim, and Running Water was bandaging up the Sheriff's injuries from the cougar. And the Sheriff complained the whole time they are wrapping his arm.

"When are we leaving to go get the artifacts, Jim?" asks the Sheriff.

"In a couple of hours, we want to get there just before daybreak so we can sneak on to the reservation without being seen. Then we can look for the treasure cave."

After the Sheriff is patched up, the three men get into a jeep and head for the reservation to steal more artifacts to sell. After surgery, Dr. Fox and Dr. Tall Elk wake up Dennis and Little Bird.

"Wake up; it's early morning. And Dr. Fox tells me you have an amazing story for me."

Dennis wakes up, stretches and yawns, so does Little Bird. Dennis takes his book and hands it to Dr. Tall Elk.

"What it all boils down to is I discovered this cave, and it had this talking stick in it."

Dennis shows him the picture.

"Three men attacked us and took the talking stick, and I hope we can catch them before they do any other harm."

"I see. Let's see the Chief. Then you can tell the Chief all about it, said Tall Elk.

Tall Elk calls the Chief, hangs up the phone, and hustles everyone over to the Chief's house. Once they are all assembled, Dr. Tall Elk makes introductions, then has Dennis launch into his story. Dennis tells of the cougar attack, and the trek to save Little Bird, and the cave and what he found. Then the time spent with Little Bird at the hospital. And about the three men who stole the talking stick and Dennis's sketchbook. Then Dennis gives the pictures to the Chief to look at. Dr. Fox backs up all that Dennis said, and so does Little Bird. Dr. Tall Elk tells the Chief about the surgery that Dr. Fox did for the Chief's granddaughter. The Chief walks over to his telephone and places several calls, then motions everyone to follow him to the meeting hall. By this time, the sun is just coming up over the mountains. And the three men are already on the reservation searching for the artifacts following the talking stick's clues. At the first location on the back trail shown by the map on the stick, they find three holes, and only one of them is the proper hole. (*What they need was the chant that Little Bird knows to know which hole to pick*) The men chose the wrong hole, and the trap is sprung, and the Sheriff gets badly injured, with his leg broken. And he lays there screaming. Jim and Running Water try to quiet him down, or the Tribal police will catch them. They soon secure his leg by using his coat, and then his shirt cut into strips to tie some branches along his leg, then give him his wallet to bite on. Then Jim and Running Water take the Talking stick and continue. With a promise to return and get the Sheriff and bring him back home. Now that the tribe is alerted to the thieves' possible presents, they search the reservation looking for them.

The Sheriff is the first one found, and the tribal policeman radios the location, then leaves the Sheriff to follow the trail of the other two men. Soon another tribal lawman is walking upon the Sheriff when the Sheriff pulls his gun and threatens to shoot anyone who comes near him.

"No problem, Sheriff, we'll leave you but don't be surprised at the critters you'll attract, and your gun may not be enough to protect you. Also, you appear to be badly hurt. We can take you to the clinic and at least give you something for the pain."

"Alright, I give up. The pain is too much."

The Sheriff throws the gun to the feet of the tribal Lawman and puts up his hands. The Lawman waves his hand, and a dozen men appear with guns. They put the Sheriff on a litter and carry him to the clinic to be treated.

CHAPTER SEVENTEEN

Once the Sheriff is on his way, the remaining eight men follow the trail, and Jim and Running Water walk to the next place on the Talking stick map. Jim and Running Water hunt around for the set of three holes, and they locate them on a boulder. Jim puts the Talking stick into the hole. The tribal policeman calls out not to put the stick into the hole, and Running Water shoots at him, causing the policeman to duck for cover. The policeman does not return fire, but he warns them not to put the stick into the hole. Jim does not listen and jams the Talking stick into the wrong hole, causing a boulder from up above to dislocate and roll down the hill, and it slams into Jim, knocking him off the cliff and crushing his chest, leaving Running Water by himself. Drop your gun Running Water, you are surrounded, and they all have rifles pointed at you. Someone from hiding shoots at Running Waters feet, so he throws down his gun.

"Alright, I surrender." He holds up his hands.

One of the men comes up and pats down Running Water looking for other weapons, and finds none.

"He's clean!" shouts the Tribal Policeman.

Running Water gets handcuffed, and the policeman recovers the Talking stick and marches them back along the trail until they find the Chief and his party.

The policeman hands the Talking stick to the Chief, who hands it to the tribes new Shaman, and he looks over the Talking stick, and he hums the chant that little Bird sang for him.

"We must start at the beginning, or we will lose everything."

They all return to the first place where the Sheriff got hurt and the Shaman starts doing the chant, as the shaman chants, he puts the stick into the correct hole, and they can hear or see nothing, then a slight trembling shakes the area. They were expecting an earthquake when it started, but nothing more happened. They press on to the following location where Jim was killed, and the shaman again sings the chant and places the Talking stick into the correct hole. And again a slight trembling occurs, then stops. They move on to the last location, where the shaman does the final chant and puts the Talking stick into the proper hole to unlock the final secret. The ground trembles and a large boulder rolls loose and bounces down the hill, and falls into the canyon, opening a cave entrance.

"Let's go see what wonders we have before us," said the shaman.

The shaman enters the cave first and sees three pathways to take; he looks at the Talking stick and sees that the right fork is marked. Standing behind them is the Chief and Little Bird, then Running Water. Just as they start down the path Running Water breaks free and runs to the left fork, hoping to getaway. No one follows him, and soon they hear a scream, and it dies in the distance.

"I have been here before when I was very young. Said the Chief, as I recall, there is a steep drop off into a pit." the Chief remarks.

They walk along down the right passage and come to an open chamber. All around them are all kinds of artifacts; there is even some gold and silver.

"Little Bird, thank you and your friend Dennis; you have returned our heritage to us. You may now return to your tribe in honor."

Little Bird hugs the Chief and starts crying. The Chief lifted her face and brushed away her tears.

"What is wrong Little Bird?"

"Nothing, I have looked so long for the Talking stick and to have it all end. It makes me happy."

"Nobody touch anything here, leave it where it is; we will want pictures to give our new friend Dennis; after all, without his help, we wouldn't be here this day."

The tribal law officers are left in charge to guard the cave. And in an hour, someone shows up to take pictures of the cave for Dennis. Dennis couldn't go on this part of the expedition due to his injury, and when they all returned to the Chief's home, they tell Dennis all that happened. The whole time Little Bird held Dennis's hand. By evening the pictures are done, and they are given to Dennis.

"Young man, you will spend the night with us, and you'll see all the artifacts as they are put into our museum. You'll see what you have restored to us."

"Thank you, Chief I'd like that very much."

As promised, the Chief help Dennis to the museum the following day to see all the artifacts being brought in, and placed on the shelves and in cases. By the end of the day, Dennis has seen everything and can make all the artifacts' sketches he wants. Dr. Fox comes to Dennis and informs him that they must return home. But before they go, the Chief makes Dennis and Dr. Fox members of the tribe. Dennis gets help to Dr. Fox's car, and then Dennis gets helped into the car. Little Bird is standing there and is blushing. Dennis looks up and smiles when she puts her arms around his neck and kisses him. Then she turns and runs away. The Chief chuckles.

"A to be young again and in love." As the chief places his hand on Dennis's shoulder. He chuckles again.

Chapter Eighteen

"Ready to leave Dennis?"

"I guess so, Dr. Fox."

Dr. Fox starts the car to take Dennis home.

"Little Bird cannot read, can she, Dr. Fox?"

"No, Dennis, she can't, or at least not yet."

"That's why she couldn't bring me the right book."

"That's right, Dennis, and that's why I stopped you. You would've made her feel ashamed; then she would've hated you."

"Thank you! I believe I love that girl."

"We all saw that, and I hope what follows will be well. Little Bird loves you too, by the way."

"Thanks, for that Dr. Fox."

On the way home, Dr. Fox asks many questions more to pass the time than anything. It seems to be very soon, and we are at my house getting helped out by Dr. Fox and my brother into the house. Dr. Fox opens the bandage and then cleans the wound again and bandages it up.

"Dennis, you should be able to get up and around by the end of the week, then you can go back to school."

"Thank you."

After Dr. Fox leaves, I'm pummeled by questions from everyone all at once. So, I ask them to all be quiet and that I would start from the day we left. So, I told them all that happened. And that I was now a part of the Nez Peirce tribe. The days blend, and I write a letter or two to Little Bird hoping someone would read it to her. I graduated from high school and off to the Navy to fulfill my three years of being in the military. While there, I managed to make a large sum of money doing sketches. I sketched the Ship's Captain with the Ship in the background. Everyone was so impressed that I was doing all the officers and some of the crew. I almost got into trouble with the people in Photo for stealing their customers. Somehow my sketches got to the fleet magazine, and The Navy News was having me do drawings for their newspaper. In between times, I sent a letter to Little Bird. She never answered them. I just figured she did not know how to write.

My time was up, and I left the Navy, But the Navy News still wants me to make sketches for them, and so I'm hired as a civilian to do the drawings. I make it back home to visit and see if I might borrow the car to see Little Bird. Mom gives me her keys, and she has this look like You will have to see for yourself because you won't believe me if I tell you. I drive to the Nez Pearce Indian reservation as I get to the check-in station to ask if they can locate Little Bird. the Man at the gate.

"Hey, you're him."

"What?" I ask.

"You're Dennis, aren't you?"

"Yes, I am."

"I'm glad to meet you. And by the way, Dr. Tall Elk wants to see you as soon as you got here."

"Is he at the clinic?" I ask

"Yes, he knew you were coming."

I thank the young man and drive to the clinic and go inside. I'm on pins and needles, wondering what's going on. Dr. Tall Elk meets me in the waiting room.

Chapter Nineteen

"Hi Dennis, it's so good to see you!"

He shakes my hand.

"Here, sit down, can we talk for a few minutes."

"Ok, I said, what do you want to talk about?"

"There's no easy way to say this, but Little Bird is married and has a little boy and another child on the way; she's married."

My soul and heart crash right there. What did I do wrong to lose her? I think.

"Dennis, it's not what you think; Little Bird loves you beyond words. She did what she did for the sake of her children."

"I don't understand!"

"I didn't think you would. Little Bird didn't want her children to go through life, always being picked on because they would be half-breed. Neither belonging to the White man or Indian worlds. Both worlds would shun them. She understood that and gave you up for the children's sake, instead of her happiness."

"I guess I can respect that. Well, I understand what my mother wanted to tell me. I guess I had best return to my family. Bye, Tall Elk."

"Hold on a moment; I have someone important I want you to meet."

"Nurse, call Jackson to the main desk."

The call is made, and a young Indian man comes up to the desk.

"Yes, Dr. Tall Elk."

"Jackson, meet Dennis."

They shake hands, "The Dennis."

"Yes Jackson, the Dennis."

Jackson pumps Dennis's hand and almost won't let it go.

"What makes me so special, Doc?"

"Well, Dennis, you have become something of a legend around here."

"Why, I haven't done anything?"

"No, Dennis, you help return our past to us through your efforts, and there is something of a love story going on here as well."

"Dennis, I married Little Bird, but after meeting you. I wish she had married you instead."

"Why?"

"Because she truly loves you. I try to do all I can to make her happy. And I think she is; I know she loves the children. In my heart, I know she pines for you. But will not show it to me."

"Jackson, I can tell you are a good man, and if she is happy. Then I'll be happy. It's nice to have met you. May you always make one another happy."

Jackson smiles at me, and I can tell he knows I hurt.

"Thank you, Dennis, and I mean it."

"Well, Guys, it is a long way home; I'd best get started."

Both men shake my hand, and I turn to leave. With a heavy heart, I return home.

"I see from the facial expression you found out about Little Bird and that she is married."

"I did, and I met her husband Jackson; he is very nice. He was going to ask me to come to dinner, but I left before he could. Well, Mom, tomorrow I will go to Spokane and see if I can find a place to live and start a new life."

Chapter Twenty

The following month was a blur getting a house to live in, getting established, and sending out my address to the companies I'll be working for. I continue to look into the Nez Pearce Indians' history. And I go to the main library to do my research. One day I see a woman reading a story to many children, and I listen in. it was a pleasant diversion. Over time the librarian comes to know me and watches me do my sketches. And after a time, I let her see them, and she talks me into hanging them about the room.

I was working away at one of my sketches when the librarian came up to me and asked.

"Dennis, our storybook reader is sick today, and would you be willing to step in and help us by doing a story?"

"I don't know, what story?"

"Any story, make one up about your sketches. The Children will love it."

I sit back and think about it.

"Ok, I'll do it. I have a true story, and I have all the sketches to go with it."

"Thank you, Dennis, it will be in an hour. Will you be ready?"

"For this story, I could do it this minute."

The time arrives, and Dennis is seated in the storyteller's chair, and the children are seated around him. And he sees that the ages vary from five years old to ten years old. And he hopes he can keep their attention as he tells them his story.

"Ok, children, I'm your storyteller today, and I hope we all can get along."

Dennis sees some of them fidgeting. He thinks he will lose them in a few minutes, so he changes how he will deliver his story.

"Now listen up, I'm going to tell you a true story, filled with true love, adventure, danger, thieves, and Indians."

Looking around the room, he sees the fidgeting stop, and everyone's eyes are on Dennis. As he tells his story using his sketchbook at the end of the hour. There wasn't a dry eye in the place. Some of the young girls came up to Dennis and hugged him. The librarian came to Dennis and asked if he would like to retell his story to others? Dennis agrees.

Two weeks later, Dennis is up to tell his story to some older kids, tweens, and teens from a nearby school. Even the storyteller is there. One other group of people came that Dennis did not see, and that was little Bird and her family.

Dennis launches into this story and uses the sketchbook as before to help tell his story. When he finishes, not a single person had a dry eye, epically the girls. From out of the crowd, Little Bird stands up and walks over to Dennis and gives him a big hug; her husband is standing there laughing and holding the baby and the hand of their little boy. Little Bird was so choked up she couldn't talk. Jackson is all smiles and gives a hearty laugh.

"Dennis, that was the best true story I have ever heard. I bet I could book you at the next tribal meeting to tell that story. It was pure delight, thank you!"

Little Bird had a hard time letting go of Dennis, but she does. One of the teens asks Little Bird.

"Are you Little Bird?"

"Yes, I am."

"Why didn't you marry Dennis?"

"You heard his story; all that Dennis said was true."

"Do you still love him?"

"Yes, I do love Dennis; you are young, yet when you grow up and have a family, you will understand what I did. You see, I love my family too, my children and my husband."

"Little Bird, who invited you here?"

"That was my doing, Dennis. Said the librarian. After your first story, I started digging, and I located Little Bird and her family. I decided to invite them, and you see they came."

"I guess I should thank you. But I'm not sure I should."

"You should, thank her, Dennis. It was the greatest gift I've ever received. You bring the best out of people;

you brought the best out of me. And you gave me such courage. You've shown me White people can be very good. And I thank you for that. My family and I must be going. Dennis, Goodbye!"

That was the last time I saw Little Bird and her family. I moved on with my life, and I married the librarian, and we have a couple of children of our own, a girl and a boy.

THE END